KNIGHTS
PANTERRA IN PERIL

BRECKLAN

DINO KNIGHTS
PANTERRA IN PERIL

JEFF NORTON
ILLUSTRATED BY JEFF CROSBY

Scallywag Press Ltd
LONDON

Text first self published by Jeff Norton, 2019

This new edition first published in Great Britain
in 2021 by Scallywag Press Ltd,
10 Sutherland Row, London SW1V 4JT

Printed and bound in Great Britain by Short Run Press Limited

Printed on FSC paper

001

British Library Cataloguing in Publication Data available

ISBN 978-1-912650-73-6

Brecklan Sea

Horn Hills

IV

III

II

I

Roaring Ocean

BRECKLAN

I   Harding Manor

II The Great Lawn

III Brecklan Town

IV Brecklan Berry Fields

V   Salterius' Hideaway

VI Sir Neville Avingdon's Castle

You are about to meet...

Galliard

Torin

Elspeth

Iyla

Henry

THE DINO KNIGHTS

Galliard

Torin

Elspeth

Iyla

Henry

Lord Harding
Longtime ruler
of Brecklan,
and Henry's
guardian.

Lady Anwyn
Wise co-ruler
of Brecklan, and
champion
of peace.

Sir Neville Avingdon
Evil master of the Swamp
States, with his eye on
conquering Brecklan.

Krilla
Chief Guard
of the Swamp
States, known for
her strength and
ruthlessness.

Queen Ignis
Mysterious queen
of Volcanica,
a neutral state
in Panterra.

Salterius
A kindly, old
inventor, now
banished from
Brecklan.

Henry Fairchild woke to the sound of
a ginormous growl. He rubbed his
tummy – he didn't feel *that* hungry! Then
there was a snort and another growl.
The noises were coming from the stables
below his bed in the loft.

I know what they want, he thought,
easing himself off the thin mattress.

He stood up beneath the eaves, remembering just in time to duck his head. He'd hit his forehead on the loft beams too many times to count and had the bruises to prove it.

Climbing down the rickety ladder, he held his breath against the stench of soiled straw. He jumped from the last step and landed softly on the dirt floor. Turning round, he gazed down the row of animal pens.

"Everybody, up!"

The dinosaurs shifted in their pens, heads twitching at the sound of his voice. They all knew what those words meant – breakfast! Ever since he was a small child, Henry had had a special relationship with the dinos of Brecklan. That's what made him such a good stable boy.

He opened the large double doors to the stables and breathed in a huge lungful of fresh morning air from the green pasture.

Henry grabbed his satchel off its hook and looped it around his shoulder. Then he opened the door of the first pen.

"Good morning, Tribus," he said.

The three-horned Triceratops grunted back at him, slowly rising from the straw. The dino bowed his head so that Henry could give each horn a quick polish with an old rag. Tribus loved to have his horns rubbed!

"Very handsome," Henry said, plucking a purple Brecklan berry from his satchel. He turned it round in his hand. Brecklan berries were like giant blueberries. Henry held it out on the flat of his palm for Tribus to eat. The dinosaur snaffled up the berry and licked Henry's hand clean, the rough surface of his tongue tickling so that Henry squirmed and laughed.

After Henry gave him a gentle smack on his giant bottom, Tribus lumbered out of his pen, heading towards the pasture.

Henry looked down the row of stalls. "Who's next?"

The Hypsilophodon rose up on her hind legs, showing Henry her soft, white belly. Hyppy purred with contentment as Henry scratched her scales. Henry grabbed another berry and tossed it into the air. Hyppy snatched it before scurrying out to join Tribus in the pasture. Henry fondly watched her leave. Feeding time was the best time!

One by one, Henry greeted his animals and sent them out of the stables. The dinos were about twice Henry's height. He'd heard stories that, in ancient times, wild dinosaurs could be as tall as a castle. But over the generations, Brecklan's dinosaurs had been bred to be smaller than their ancestors. The Brecklan berries made them friendly and tame, so that the dinosaurs lived harmoniously with humans.

In Panterra's other provinces, the dinosaurs were still wild, huge and dangerous. It was only in the tiny province of Brecklan that dinos lived side by side with people.

Finally, Henry arrived at the smallest pen, housing the smallest dino – Henry's favourite friend, Bounce. Bounce was covered in feathers. They trembled whenever Bounce was nervous – which meant they trembled a lot. As soon as Henry opened Bounce's pen, the creature nuzzled his head into Henry's chest. Bounce had a round body that wobbled on top of skinny legs. Henry thought he looked more like a chicken than a dinosaur, though he'd never tell Bounce that. Henry ruffled Bounce's colourful feathers and the animal let out a *chirp-chirp*. Henry rewarded him with a berry, patting his flank and sending him out to join the others.

He started to muck out the pens, scooping out quivering piles of fresh dino poop to load into a wooden wheelbarrow. Henry took hold of the handles and wheeled it to the bottom of the field where he tipped the manure onto a compost heap that steamed in the cool morning air. The stench made his eyes water! But waste not, want not – the dino poop would fertilise the most important crop in the province – Brecklan berries.

Henry returned the wheelbarrow and tidied up the stables, finally turning his mind to his own breakfast. He walked towards the servants' entrance at the rear of the imposing stone mansion. His tummy rumbled. *I hope Cook's saved me some sausages!* But as he passed the front of the stately home, curiosity got the better of him.

Despite the early hour, a carriage was waiting on the gravel drive of Harding Manor. The household staff – including

Cook and the steward – were lined up to see it off. Henry definitely wouldn't be getting any sausages today. What were they all doing out here?

Lord Harding and Lady Anwyn appeared at the grand entrance. Working in the stables, Henry hardly ever saw the lord and lady – he opened his mouth to greet them, then snapped it shut. *Never speak unless spoken to.* He'd better not chance it.

Lord Harding's silver hair shone in the morning sunlight, his tall figure stooped over a cane made from polished dinosaur bone. Beside him, Lady Anwyn wore a ruby-coloured cloak. She pulled down the hood and lifted her face to the misty morning. Her dark hair was pulled back in a bun kept in place with a long dinosaur tooth. Together, they approached their shiny black carriage. As always, it was being pulled by two Parasaurolophuses.

Lady Anwyn noticed Henry. "Oh, there's Henry! Hello, young man."

He was allowed to speak now.

"Good morning," called Henry, stooping to offer a bow.

She and Harding had always been kind to Henry, but most of the time he lived in the care of the steward, Arthur. From his place in the row of servants, Arthur glared at Henry.

"I hope it is," said Lord Harding, glancing nervously towards the south.

Despite Arthur's glares, Henry dared to come closer. "Where are you going so early?" he asked.

Arthur cleared his throat, narrowing his eyes at Henry to tell him to be quiet.

"Brecklan state affairs," replied Lord Harding.

That could mean anything! Henry thought.

Henry knew that Lord Harding and Lady Anywn worked hard to keep Brecklan safe and prosperous. They often hosted important people at the manor house and even threw grand balls to make the visiting officials feel important. Henry liked to listen to the music, but it sometimes spooked the dinosaurs.

Lady Anwyn whispered, "There's been talk of a battle looming on the southern border. We want to negotiate before conflict breaks out."

"Indeed," said Lord Harding. "But talk

cannot always prevent war."

"War?" gasped Henry.

He'd heard a few of the servants talking lately about other provinces battling for control over Panterra. They had been worried the conflict might spill over into Brecklan, which was a peaceful place.

The sound of galloping filled the air. Four armoured knights riding dinosaurs rounded the mansion. Dino Knights! Up till now, Henry had only ever glimpsed the Dino Knights in parades and tournaments! They were brave and strong warriors – he dreamed of being just like them.

Henry's mouth hung open as he watched the dinos trotting towards the carriage. He recognised a teenage girl with short black hair, who rode a knobbly Ankylosaur. That was Iyla. She winked at Henry as she passed.

Another dinosaur sped past her. This one was famous for his speed and ability to mimic bird calls. The Ornithomimus was ridden by Galliard, a tall lad with long locks of golden hair. Brightly coloured silks peeked out from beneath his polished silver armour. He pulled his dino up to Lord Harding and gave a theatrical bow. Gally took no notice of Henry, but Henry didn't take offence. Everyone knew that Gally never took notice of anyone other than himself.

By his side rode Elspeth. She sat high in the saddle on her spiky Styracosaurus. Elspeth – Ellie for short – had curly red hair.

Pulling up at the rear was Torin, their leader. He was handsome, with a chiselled jaw and a warm smile that he flashed at Henry. He rode a well-groomed Nothronychus that trotted on two legs.

"Dino Knights at your service, my lord, my lady," Torin said, steering his dino to the front of the group. He turned to gaze down at Henry. "My squire."

Squire? Henry had never been called that before.

Gally gave a snort. "Hardly! A mere poop-scooper."

Henry felt his cheeks burn with shame.

"We all do our bit for Brecklan," interrupted Lord Harding. "You on the field of battle, and Henry in the stables.

Maybe a stint of mucking out would build your character, Galliard."

Ellie laughed. "I'd give up a week of puddings to see that!"

Gally glared at Henry. Had Henry just made an enemy?

The four knights surrounded the carriage as Lord Harding climbed up and took the reins. A servant helped his wife up after him.

Lord Harding looked around at the knights and raised his voice. "We ride…"

The knights responded in unison, "For Brecklan!" This was the Dino Knights' famous call to action – everyone in the province knew it off by heart.

The two Parasaurolophuses leapt forward, and the Dino Knights took their positions: two in front and two behind. Henry watched the carriage move down the long drive as the servants waved and cheered. They rode over the moat bridge and onto the main road south, disappearing as quickly as they'd arrived.

As always, Henry was left behind in his little corner of Brecklan. He felt his tummy tighten with longing. *Will I ever see more of the province?* Was it all too much to hope for?

"That's enough loafing about!" called Arthur.

With a sinking heart, Henry pushed his dream aside. He turned to face the steward, who was holding out a shovel as if to remind Henry of his place in the realm.

"Don't be too envious, lad," he said. "I hear there's a wild T-Rex on the rampage in the forests to the south."

Henry's jaw dropped as he looked down the south road where the carriage had gone. "Why didn't you warn them?"

"Not my business," said the steward. "They only employ me to keep the grounds clean."

Henry took the shovel as Arthur and the rest of the servants disappeared back inside the mansion.

Henry looked at the distant silhouette of the carriage. A rampaging T-Rex? Lord Harding and Lady Anwyn could be hurt or – worse – killed!

He thought quickly, calculating the distance. If he could just... He glanced at Bounce, who was grazing on a patch of rhododendron. *Yes, he might be quick enough.*

After checking that Arthur was nowhere to be seen, Henry raced back to the stables. He gazed around wildly.

Think, Henry, think! What do you need?

His eyes lit on a spare set of tack hanging from a nail driven into a wall. That might come in useful. He plucked the glossy leather reins and saddle off the nail and ran out into the pasture. Henry put his fingers to his lips and let out a long, high whistle – his familiar call to his favourite dino. In response, Bounce cantered across the pasture, his flanks heaving.

Henry saw the top of the carriage moving behind a hedge before it disappeared out of sight. "Come on!"

Bounce stood patiently as Henry clambered up onto a set of stone steps hewn especially for short humans wanting to ride dinosaurs. Bounce's feathers felt soft beneath his hands, but they seemed to glow with an energy as though Henry's friend understood the urgency of their mission.

He raised his fist in the air, just like he'd seen the Dino Knights do, and Bounce gave a roar of approval. It was now or never. "We ride for Brecklan!"

II

Henry gripped the reins tightly in his fists as Bounce whipped through the woods, down a short cut that led to the Swamp States. Left, right, left! They swerved between the trees. The two of them moved fluidly together, as though they'd been born to do this.

As they moved further south, a roar filled the forest and Henry gave a shudder. Bounce sensed Henry's fear and slowed down.

"No, come on. We have to keep going!" Henry dug his heels into the dino's flanks. The words had barely left his mouth when—

Roar!

Bounce slowed down again as Henry felt prickles travel over his skin. 'What was that?' he whispered. Almost in answer came an even louder…

ROAR!

It sounded like a dinosaur. A very *angry* dinosaur. Bounce broke into a canter and burst through the trees.

Ahead of them, a dirt highway carved through the forest. In the distance, Henry spotted the carriage – with a Tyrannosaurus Rex blocking its path.

The beast was about three times Henry's height. He roared with fury at the four Dino Knights protecting the carriage. Torin and Iyla stood up on their stirrups, swords held aloft. Ellie and Gally had come round to flank them on either side. Henry couldn't make out even the tiniest glimpse of fear. The Dino Knights were unstoppable! Weren't they…?

The beast bellowed again and reared up to his full height. Was he going to charge? Henry had to do something!

But what?

Torin and Iyla thrust their swords out to warn off the beast, but the T-Rex swiped his tail, knocking the other dinos off their feet. He looked ready to pounce when

Ellie and Gally rushed forwards, slicing their swords through the air. But the Rex gave another furious roar, his eyes wild. They were making things worse!

Henry leapt off Bounce and ran straight for the T-Rex. He tore open his satchel. If swords didn't work, maybe berries could! He dug out a handful and scattered Brecklan berries on the ground, hoping to tempt the dinosaur away from the carriage. But as the T-Rex turned to roar at Henry, he slammed a terrible, giant foot into the berries, squishing them to pulp.

"Poop-scooper!" cried Gally, as he spotted Henry. "What are you doing here?"

"Get out of here, lad!" shouted Torin, waving to him to get away. "It's not safe."

"You'll get yourself killed!" Ellie's face was pale. Bounce retreated behind the other dinosaurs.

Henry didn't blame his dino for being scared. Neither of them had ever seen a T-Rex up close. His fangs dripped with saliva and Henry could see ancient scars on his hide that looked like war wounds. From sword blades? Henry wondered if the creature had fought with humans before. But no matter how the T-Rex had got those scars, he had survived – and he was furious.

"Get out of the way, Henry!" came a shout. Lord Harding kicked open the carriage door and leapt out, a gleaming silver sword in his hand. He braced himself, the varnished oak of his wooden leg glistening in the sunshine. "I'll settle this in the only way a beast understands!"

"My lord!" Henry called over the T-Rex's outraged roar. "Put down your sword." He swallowed, remembering this was the lord of the manor. "Please."

"I'll do no such thing," Harding barked, his hand tightening around the hilt. "I lost my leg to one of these monsters. Now I shall even the score."

"NO!" Henry ran to stop him. Lord Harding's eyes widened in shock. Clearly, he hadn't heard the word "No" in a long time. "With respect, Sir, I don't think you are in danger. Look at the dino's side."

Lord Harding glanced at the creature's old wounds. "What of it?"

"I think those are sword scars. This Rex feels threatened."

The beast roared again, his rancid breath sweeping over Henry.

"All of you," Henry said. "Lay down your weapons." He didn't care who he was issuing orders to now – he wouldn't see a living thing harmed. Not when they didn't deserve it.

"Are you crazy?" called Torin.

"We'll be eaten alive!" said Gally.

"I could blind it with a smoke bomb," offered Iyla. She scrambled around in her satchel and pulled out what looked like a ball of dirt. "Then, Torin, you strike with your sword!"

Hadn't any of them heard a word he'd said? Henry looked over at the Rex and held his hands out, palms up, to show he had no weapons. Keeping his eyes trained on the dinosaur, he motioned to the others.

"Put your weapons down," he whispered.

They each looked at Lord Harding for permission. He hesitated, then gave a small nod. Reluctantly, they each bent down to slowly place their weapons on the ground.

The T-Rex snorted, nostrils flaring. If he was going to attack, it would be now. But he didn't make a move. Henry slowly gestured for the Rex to sit and the giant creature lowered its flanks. He understood him! Henry looked into the dinosaur's yellow eyes, forcing himself not to blink. He felt his heart beat slow down.

"That's right, Rex," said Henry, never breaking eye contact. "We're not going to hurt you."

"Incredible," said Harding.

"I told you," came Lady Anwyn's voice from the carriage. "He has a gift."

Henry called back to the group. "You see, he means you no harm."

"Those teeth are telling me different," said Ellie.

The T-Rex lowered his head to Henry's level and let out a strange, low sound – almost like a purr. Henry reached out to stroke the animal's scales, just above his jaw. His hide felt rough and weathered beneath his hand.

"My word," muttered Lord Harding. "But…but I thought Tyrannosaurs were untameable."

"So did I," admitted Henry. "But this one, well, he seems to…respect me."

Gally snorted with derision. "A *stable* boy?"

Henry felt his cheeks flush with anger. What was wrong with being a stable boy?

As if sensing Henry's anger, the T-Rex raised his head and growled at Gally.

"Careful, Gally," said Ellie. "This stable boy has made a powerful new friend."

"More than one," said Lord Harding, walking to Henry's side. Lady Anwyn climbed out of the carriage to join them.

"You saved us, Henry," she said. "Do you know what this means?" She glanced over at the four others, who'd watched helplessly as Henry had mastered a T-Rex, all on his own. "You must join the Dino Knights."

Henry looked from face to outraged face. He could not believe his ears. He felt a swell of pride and began to open his mouth to thank her ladyship, when—

"No doubt," Gally said, "the beast smelt the funk of its own kind on this boy. Stable stench does stay with one."

I'll show them, thought Henry. He motioned to the T-Rex to kneel down and then clambered up his tail and onto his back. The carnivore rose on his hind legs and Henry looked down at the others from a great height.

"It would be an honour to serve you," said Henry. He'd join the Dino Knights, whether they liked it or not.

Lord Harding stared, open-mouthed. No one had ever ridden a T-Rex. He caught the satisfied look on the face of Lady Anwyn.

"Oh, very well," Harding said. "I will allow him to train."

The other knights shared glances, their cheeks reddening, but they knew better than to defy Lord Harding.

Henry smiled. "So, I'm going to be a Dino Knight?"

"If you have what it takes," said Torin. "But right now, we have a mission to finish – to escort the lord and lady to the peace talks."

Henry looked over at Bounce. "Run on home, boy," Henry said. He knew Bounce liked to feel useful, so Henry gave him a job. "I need you to look after the rest of the herd now that I'm gone."

Responsibility! That did the trick. Bounce lumbered happily back through the woods as the knights gathered their weapons and climbed back onto their dinos. Henry touched the T-Rex on his right side, and the creature turned towards the Dino Knights. He was learning quickly! Then, together they escorted the carriage along the highway, trotting south towards the Swamp States.

Riding on the T-Rex, Henry felt powerful and nervous at the same time.

Torin moved to ride alongside him. "Well played, lad," he said. "You may be riding a carnivore, but don't forget, I'm still leader of this pack."

"Of course," Henry said. He wasn't here to pick a fight – he just wanted to help.

He gently rubbed the T-Rex's back, causing him to slow down, and Henry took up the rear behind the carriage. Henry squared his shoulders as he glanced around at the hills and valleys of the kingdom stretching away to the horizon. He liked the view from up high. For the first time in his life, riding alongside the Dino Knights, he felt part of something. Something big. Something thrilling. Something dangerous…

III

Henry gazed around a giant clearing in the forest. His limbs were tired but his face was flushed with excitement – riding a giant T-Rex was the best adventure he'd ever had. The two of them had quickly learnt how to move together and understand each other's signals.

After travelling south for hours, the group had finally arrived at the agreed meeting place between Brecklan and the Swamp States. It was a clearing in the forest, a long rectangle where trees had been felled. Henry would never have found this place on his own.

"Why are we meeting in the middle of the forest?" he asked, gazing around. "There's nothing here."

"Exactly," Lord Harding said from his carriage. "Neutral ground. Or, at least, that's the theory."

At the far end of the clearing, Henry spotted a pair of huge, wooden seats facing each other. Etched into the wood were creatures of the forest. The seats looked almost like thrones. They were guarded by a warrior woman wearing

a necklace of razor-sharp raptor teeth. Her armour looked as though it was made out of tough dino skins. Over one shoulder, she rested a club fashioned from a dinosaur's leg bone.

Henry shuddered. *She looks terrifying!*

Lord Harding climbed out of his carriage and leant on his cane as he walked over.

"Who are you?" he asked.

"Krilla, Chief Guard of the Swamp States," she said. "You're late."

"So is Neville Avingdon," said Harding, looking around.

The Dino Knights steered their dinos to surround the meeting place, protecting their master. Henry and Rex held back. Henry peered off between the trees, unable to shake the feeling that they weren't entirely alone.

"He will be along shortly," Krilla said. "Sit."

To Henry, it sounded more like an order than an offer, but Harding took a seat on one of the massive wooden thrones.

From above, Henry heard a *whoosh*. He looked up to see a large bird circling. As it flapped its wings and let out a screech, Henry quickly realised it wasn't a bird at all.

"A Pterosaur," he gasped.

"I've never seen one so close," he heard Iyla say.

Pterosaurs were wild, migratory beasts that lived to the far east of Brecklan.

The creature glided lower, its massive wings casting a shadow over them. She had a long beak and skin that looked mottled and grey. As she descended along the length of the clearing, Henry saw the silhouette of a man riding her, his legs astride the Pterosaur's neck. The animal swooped down, down, down… She looked as though she was going to crash into them, but at the last moment she swerved off to land beside the thrones. The Pterosaur dug her claws into the ground, bracing her legs, so that the rider nearly tipped over her head onto the ground.

"Neville Avingdon really does like to make an entrance," said Torin.

Neville's face was hidden behind a pair of dark goggles, and a red scarf wrapped jauntily around his throat. He wore a fitted brown jacket made out of soft dino hide. As he climbed off the beast, he slapped her on the beak. "You call that a landing, Zia?"

The animal let out a meek whimper.

"Ah, you made it," Neville said, removing his goggles and pulling down his scarf to reveal a thin moustache and a broad smile. His eyes ranged over the group before pausing on Henry's T-Rex. "My goodness, you Brecks must have cultivated some powerful new berries to tame one of *those*."

He strode over to the empty throne and sat down opposite Harding. "Thank you for accepting my invitation."

"It read more like an ultimatum," replied Harding. "What do you want, Neville?"

Neville's fingertips drummed on the arm of his chair. "I'll get straight to the point. The other provinces are demanding your seeds. They want to grow their own Brecklan berries."

"Never!" Lady Anwyn called out from the carriage.

Neville didn't flinch. "If you don't hand them over," he warned, "we'll take them for ourselves."

"Our berries don't grow outside of Brecklan soil," said Harding, looking his opponent in the eye. "Everyone knows that."

"Then you should hope," Neville replied with a cruel smile, "that the other provinces don't invade your land."

Henry felt a shiver of fear race through him. Invade his province? The only home he'd ever known? He couldn't let that happen!

"They'd have to go through us," said Iyla, shifting in her saddle.

"The Dino Knights," scoffed Krilla. "So patriotic. It's adorable."

Harding stood up to leave. "I've had enough of this."

"Wait," said Neville. "I agree. Invasions are so…unpleasant. First, why don't we try to decide this with a tournament? Krilla's best athletes to compete against your Dino Knights. You can even host in Brecklan, if you wish."

"We'd crush them, my lord," said Ellie.

"Challenge accepted," said Lord Harding. "Come to us in two days' time."

"Forty-eight hours to prepare?" Neville rubbed his hands together. "I do like a challenge."

But as Harding climbed back into the

carriage, he whispered to the knights. "He's up to something. I don't trust him to play fair." He raised his voice, calling over the clearing. "We ride…"

"For Brecklan!" the knights cried.

"For Brecklan!" Henry joined in, pressing his feet against the T-Rex's sides.

Together, they charged back into the woods to take the dirt highway north to their home. Henry dared a final glance back over his shoulder. The silhouette of Neville's Pterosaur hovered in the air above them, casting a black shadow. Neville and Krilla stood alone in the clearing, their heads close together as they talked. So why did Henry still feel as though they were being watched?

IV

Henry rolled over, half asleep. Usually the mattress rustled with straw beneath his body as he moved. His body stilled. No rustle. Something was different.

He patted the sheet, feeling his fingers sink into the soft, squidgy surface. Soft? Squidgy? He felt beneath his head.

A pillow. A plump, feather pillow. He was definitely wide awake now! He elbowed himself up and gazed around the room. There were long velvet curtains and a chandelier. His clothes were folded up neatly on a gilt chair.

Then he remembered. *I didn't sleep in the stable last night.* He rubbed a hand over his eyes. Well, Dino Knights didn't sleep in stables and… It all came flooding back!

I'm going to be a Dino Knight! He sprang out of bed and quickly got dressed in the new clothes laid out for him: dark riding trousers and a knitted shirt to wear under armour. Henry felt a wave of pride as he pulled the shirt on. It was embroidered with the crest of Brecklan, a coat of arms held aloft by two raptors.

He walked down the stairwell, passing the steward, who threw him an evil look. Henry had heard Arthur was taking over stable duties. He emerged into the courtyard. It was a cool morning, shrouded in mist.

I'm going to be a Dino Knight, he thought.

Then, out loud: "Me, a Dino Knight!"

A laugh came from behind him. It was Gally. "It takes a lot more to be a knight than taming a T-Rex and impressing the boss."

Then Gally strode out of the courtyard and onto the training field.

Rex bounded up to Henry from a different stable, one large enough for a T-Rex, and gave Henry a sticky lick that smelt of sausages. Henry followed Gally to the training field where Lord Harding was waiting for them.

Harding addressed the Dino Knights. "Let's get on with the training, shall we?" On the journey back, he'd decided that the temptation to lure Neville's knights back to their province and defeat them had been a good decision. Neville might not be trustworthy, but they'd be on safe ground in Brecklan. Wouldn't they?

Each knight took the reins of their dinosaur. Gally mounted his perfectly preened Ornithomimus. The dashing Torin climbed onto his Nothronychus. Ellie leapt onto her Styracosaurus.

"CONKER! COME BACK!" Iyla yelled as her dino meandered towards the manor house. She ran after her Ankylo and led him back, pausing beside Henry.

"We weren't properly introduced yesterday. I'm Iyla!" She held out her hand and Henry hesitantly took it. Dirt was rimed beneath her fingernails and stained her fingers. She shook his hand, pumping up and down hard, but when she released it, Henry had to fight the urge to wipe his hand down his trousers. "Sorry about that!" she added, noticing how much grease had transferred from her hand to his. "I was just tinkering with a weapon I've been designing."

Henry liked this girl and her friendly manner. "I know who you are," he said, smiling. He looked around. "I know who all of you are." Everyone in Brecklan knew about the Dino Knights, but Henry had never expected to be one of them.

"But what about you, stable boy?"

asked Ellie, as they led their dinosaurs across the field. "What's your story?"

"I'm, um…" Henry began to stutter. "I'm just Henry."

"But where did you come from?" said Iyla.

It was a question Henry wished he could answer. His earliest memories were of living in the loft of the stables, helping other stable hands clean out the muck until he was old enough to do it himself. Lord Harding and Lady Anwyn had provided for him, but they weren't his parents. He never knew his real parents and tried not to think about them because it only made him feel alone.

Lord Harding spoke up. "Henry has been here since we found him, and now

he is to train with you lot. That's all that matters."

Henry threw him a grateful look.

"Welcome to training, kid," said Torin.

"Just don't mess up," said Ellie.

"Or make us look bad," added Gally.

"WHEN YOU'RE QUITE READY!" bellowed Lord Harding, leaning on his cane. Iyla and Henry quickly mounted their dinos. "Two days from now, Avingdon and his knights come to face us in a tournament. They'll be determined to defeat us. You all know the price we'll pay if they do." He gazed around at the Dino Knights.

"What price?" Henry wondered.

Iyla leant over to whisper. "Harding would lose control over Brecklan; he'd be forced to cede it to Avingdon."

"But that's crazy," scoffed Henry.

"That is the Panterran way." Lord Harding began to hobble up and down. "The stakes are high, so we must be ready for anything. I need you to work as a team. We have two days to train. Your challenge today is to devise a system to capture the flag."

Harding pointed to the far side of the training ground where a large wooden tower topped with a red flag hid in the mist. The flag hung limp in the still air, about four storeys above the ground. Henry noticed that there was no door or steps on the structure.

"Easy!" said Iyla. A grin spread over her face. She pulled out a notebook and began to scribble in it, muttering to herself. "Just need to calculate the trajectory…multiply the weight by the force…"

She clambered off her dino, Conker, and ran over to a pile of building materials that lay beside the tower. She pulled a long plank from the pile. She was strong for someone so slight and Henry made a silent vow never to pick a fight with her.

"Conker," she said to her Ankylosaur, "a tree, please."

The squat dino lumbered into the woods and swung his club of a tail. A giant evergreen tree cracked…and groaned… and creaked…and began to fall. Right over Henry! He scrambled out of the way.

Crash!

The tree trunk exploded into the ground in a shower of splinters.

"You could have warned me!"
Henry cried.

Iyla shrugged. "Part of being a Dino
Knight is to expect the unexpected."

Conker pushed the fallen tree until
it ran alongside the tower. Then Iyla
carefully balanced the plank over
the giant log. She stood on one end,
weighing it to the ground, and waited.
The opposite side stuck up like a seesaw.

"Conker, would you do the honours?"
she said.

"Iyla, I'm not sure that's such a good
idea," said Torin.

"It's fine! I've done the maths!" She
donned her helmet and waited for her
dino. "I'll have that flag in less than ten
seconds."

Conker trundled over and swung his

tail into the air, then smashed it down on the plank.

The force of the blow sent the other end of the plank leaping into the air and Iyla catapulted into the sky.

She flew up towards the flag with a *whoosh* until her body smashed into the wooden structure and began to fall. Was she about to splat into the ground?

"**R**ex!" cried Henry. "We need to save her!"

The carnivore sprang into action. He leapt towards the tower and stretched out his thick neck to neatly catch Iyla in his mouth. Then he lowered his head to the ground and swung open his huge jaw so that Iyla rolled off his tongue, covered in sticky saliva but very much alive.

She rose to her feet and tried to shake off the spit. "Thanks, I think."

"Bad luck," Lord Harding said as she walked back to the rest of the Dino Knights.

"My turn," said Gally. "The aim is to be the one holding the flag, yes?"

Lord Harding raised an eyebrow. "If that's how you interpret the challenge."

Gally hopped off his Ornithomimus, Avin, raised his fingers to his lips and let out a shrill whistle. Avin ruffled his feathers to attention. Gally whistled again and Avin set off at a run, his wings flapping like crazy. The dino managed to heave himself into the air. The Ornithomimus didn't fly as well as Avingdon's Pterosaur, but could glide smoothly. Avin spread his wings out above their heads. Sweeping down, he caught the flag in his beak and landed elegantly next to Gally. He took a bow while the group applauded half-heartedly.

"Interesting," Lord Harding said, tapping a finger against his lips.

Torin stepped up to the front of the group. "A harder challenge would be to replace the flag." He grabbed the flag from Gally's dino and stuffed it down the back of his shirt like a cape. Henry had no idea what he intended to do.

Torin scrambled up the side of the tower, finally reaching the top and replacing the flag on its mast. Torin's dino, the Nothronychus called Haringey, looked annoyed at not being invited to help.

But Henry was impressed, if a bit jealous of Torin's prowess.

Torin climbed down the front of the tower almost as quickly and bowed to the group when he landed.

"Come on, Henry! You're up!" he said, slapping Henry on the back. "Show us what you're made of. See if you can capture the flag!"

Henry gulped. He wasn't sure what he was made of, but he reached up to whisper in the T-Rex's ear as the dino bent down to him. He had half a plan, at least.

He climbed up on Rex and spurred him on. The Tyrannosaur broke into a trot…then a canter…then a gallop.

"What's the lad got up his sleeve?" he heard Lord Harding say as they passed the group of Dino Knights.

As the two of them approached the tower, Henry slowly stood up and moved cautiously forward onto the T-Rex's head, holding his arms out for balance. He wobbled and gulped. Bracing a foot against the dino's neck, he pushed himself up, up, up until he balanced on top of Rex's head as they picked up speed. He just had to make sure he… didn't…fall…off!

"One, two, three…" he counted under his breath. Henry had to time this just right. As they reached the wooden tower, Henry called, "Now!"

Rex understood immediately. He threw his head up, tossing Henry into the air in an arc. Henry ripped the flag off the mast and waved it above his head, before realising he was now hurtling towards the ground on the other side of the tower. The air rushed past him and the flag was nearly snatched from his hands. *I don't want to die!*

Oof! He slammed hard into Rex's body. His dino had raced round to catch him. The Tyrannosaur reared up and Henry threw his arms around his new friend's scaly neck, sliding down onto his back.

"Good catch!" Henry said, giving a nudge to guide them back to the group. He couldn't believe it! He and Rex had worked so well together and he'd managed to pass the first test. He couldn't help the thrill of pride that passed over him.

"Well...it was certainly different..." Lord Harding said with a smile. Henry looked at his new team and noticed that he had earned a thumbs-up from Torin and Iyla.

Ellie took her turn at rescuing the flag and finally all the Dino Knights were done. They'd each had a go.

Lord Harding gathered the group. "Well done. You each pursued your goal individually, but…" He paused and raised his eyebrows. "You didn't work as a team. If you recall, I asked you to devise a system. *Together.* In that, you failed." His face turned serious. "This isn't a game, Dino Knights. If you're going to defend Brecklan, I need you to work together."

Henry looked at the others, doubt plunging through him. They'd shown initiative, quick thinking and strength.

They'd each tried so hard, but they hadn't understood Harding's orders. They hadn't done what their leader wanted.

Henry followed the others slowly as they wandered back towards the manor house. *Will we ever manage to work as a team?* Henry thought. Especially when he was so new to all this. And if they couldn't, how would they defend Brecklan?

In the armoury, Ellie was helping Henry into his suit of armour for the last day of training. The breastplate was dented and the steel shin protectors were a bit too big, but they would do the job.

"Now you're starting to look like one of us," said Ellie with a smile.

Henry had continued to train with the knights, learning different battle skills from each of them.

Torin taught Henry how to strike with a sword. Gally bullied Henry into what felt like countless jousting trials, but he was improving with every turn. Iyla had a different skill – she could concoct potions that exploded like magic. She mixed up strange liquids in what looked like an underground kitchen.

Today started with attack-and-deflect training. Ellie had brought her wooden staff and was showing Henry how to wield it like a weapon.

Henry tried as hard as he could. They all did. Lord Harding's words had made them each realise they had to work together. All the while, their leader watched from one of the tall manor windows. Henry couldn't tell if Harding was pleased with his progress, but at least nobody threatened to move him back to the stables.

As Henry pulled on his helmet, he thought about how far he had come from stable boy to Dino Knight. But he was worried that he'd soon have to put his skills to use in the tournament against the Swamp States.

"How am I supposed to learn everything in just two days?" wondered Henry.

"Patience, persistence and practice," Ellie told him, with a swirl of her staff. "Don't sound so downhearted. You wouldn't last one winter in the Highlands with that attitude!"

"I've never left Brecklan," said Henry, as he ducked to avoid one of Ellie's practice swipes. He straightened up. "Were you born in the Highlands?"

"Aye!" Ellie laughed. "I was raised on one of Lord Harding's farms up in the mountains. We raised dinos."

"How did you end up down here?" Henry asked.

Ellie turned to wipe the sweat from her face. "My parents were trampled in a stampede. I hid in a hidey-hole I used to play in. When Lord Harding's men found me, they brought me down here and he took me in."

Henry hadn't realised that Lord Harding had taken in other children.

"Ah, glad you could find a use for my old suit of armour, Henry!" said Gally, riding up on his steed. "It was only being used as a home for some mice. I'm glad it will see some more action."

Henry didn't much like the idea of wearing Gally's hand-me-down armour, but at least he finally had a suit of steel to call his own. He only wished his parents, whoever and wherever they were, could be here to see him suit up.

First training class over, only six more to do today. He stroked a hand down the armour. For the first time in his life, he felt like a warrior.

VI

By the next morning, the vast lawn of Harding Manor had been transformed into tournament grounds. Tiered seats on wooden stands had been erected in an oval for people to sit and watch the competition. The town band was playing, the sun shone down on the manor house and the people of Brecklan were in good spirits, looking forward to a day of jousting, battling and archery. None of them had any idea what was at stake – Lord Harding wanted it to stay a secret.

Now, Lord Harding and Lady Anwyn watched from a raised platform that was adorned with Brecklan's coat of arms and colourful flags.

"Ready?' Torin asked.

The Dino Knights gravely shook each other's hands. "Ready."

This was it. Henry felt his stomach tighten with nerves. He was fighting to save his home!

Henry and the knights rode their dinos from the stables to the north side of the tournament oval. The crowd cheered and the Dino Knights waved as though this was all a jolly day out.

Henry remembered watching many tournaments, cheering on the Dino Knights as they competed against teams from other provinces. He couldn't believe that today he was going to fight alongside them.

The crowd suddenly grew quiet. Henry spotted Krilla arrive on her raptor, proudly carrying a long staff flying the green-and-brown flag of the Swamp States. Four warriors, also riding raptors, flanked her. She planted the flag into the lawn, not caring if she tore up the turf. The crowd booed but Lord Harding patted the air to tell them to be quiet.

"Welcome!" he called out as Lady Anwyn's eyes narrowed. Henry could see her looking around for Neville, but he was nowhere to be seen. Why hadn't he accompanied his warriors here?

The tournament had been his idea in the first place!

Krilla ignored the lord's welcome, turning instead to the Dino Knights.

"For the first challenge," she declared, "we call five on five."

It was a bold call. Henry knew it was the guests' privilege to set the first challenge, but typically it would start with something civilised like jousting or archery. Krilla was calling for a brawl as the first event.

"A breach of protocol," Torin said. "But we accept." He motioned the Brecklan team to move forwards. The Dino Knights rode their dinos into the centre of the tournament grounds. This is what they'd been training for. Henry flipped down the visor on his helmet and gulped.

He suddenly didn't feel ready for this.

The five knights faced off against the five Swamp warriors. Krilla drew her club and everyone else followed suit, gripping their weapons for the fight.

Krilla's raptor sprang forwards and she swung her club at Torin. He ducked the swing as the other warriors pounced. The young man opposite Henry came at him with a large, steel sword. Rex roared, spooked by the sword, and bucked Henry off his back. Henry fell to the ground and rolled. His visor sprang open and for a brief moment he was pinned to the ground, weighed down by the heavy suit.

Looking up into the bright blue sky, he spotted two birds overhead. And then he heard them screech – a heart-wrenching sound. They weren't birds.

They were Pterosaurs. And they were swooping down towards the tournament.

Henry struggled to his feet and dived out of the way as his raptor-riding opponent barrelled down on him. All around him, swords clanged and clanked as the knights fought the warriors.

"Stop!" he yelled. "We're being attacked from above!" But with the clamour of armour, no one could hear him.

Everything seemed to go into slow motion. Henry watched as the two Pterosaurs glided down to approach the platform where Lord Harding and Lady Anwyn sat.

"Take cover!" he called. But the platform was entirely exposed and the two Pterosaurs were so close.

The crowd screamed and panicked. The Dino Knights paused in their fighting, but were too far away to help. Henry ran towards the lord and lady of the manor, but the first Pterosaur attacked, claws slicing through the air and eyes filled with fury. It swiped out a claw and in one fluid movement, tore through Lord Harding's quilted tunic and scooped him up into the air.

Harding kicked his legs and cried out wildly. Henry was too late. His master had become a tiny, dark spot in the sky, carried off by the flying beast.

He looked over to Lady Anwyn and shouted, "Duck, my lady!"

The second winged creature snatched her from her seat. She screamed as she was pulled high into the air.

"What happened?" asked Torin, riding up on Haringey.

"They just dropped out of the sky," said Henry. "They were well trained."

Torin's eyes narrowed. "The tournament was just a distraction. Lord Harding was right not to trust Neville." He turned to confront Krilla, but she and her warriors were already fleeing the tournament grounds as the crowds scattered. The Pterosaurs flapped their vast wings, disappearing to the south.

"We should chase them down," said Ellie as the four Dino Knights circled up. Rex returned and Henry climbed back into his saddle.

"This is an act of war by the Swamp States!" said Ellie.

"So…what do we do now?" asked Gally.

"I owe my life to the lord and lady," said Henry. "We have to get them back!"

VII

The Dino Knights quickly gathered supplies and weapons, then set out on their trek towards the Swamp States. After the attack from the sky, the people of Brecklan hid inside their homes.

There was no one to wave or cheer as they set out.

Instead of heading straight south, Torin suggested they flank to the east, to the volcano realm. "We need to creep up on them," he explained. "It might take longer, but it will give us an advantage."

Henry was glad of the Dino Knights' leader and his tactical training. *Maybe one day I can be as good as him.*

Before long, a large, smouldering volcano dominated the sky. The air was putrid and it stung their eyes.

"We're not in Brecklan any more," said Gally.

"Volcanica," confirmed Iyla.

"If we're spotted, we'll be mistaken for enemy soldiers," said Gally.

"Gally," teased Ellie. "We *are* enemy soldiers."

"Where exactly are we, Torin?" asked Henry.

Torin handed him a parchment map. Henry unfurled it and gulped when he saw the little etching of a volcano. He pointed. "We're in the Forbidden Zone."

The Dino Knights exchanged worried looks.

"Perhaps we should find another path," suggested Henry.

"Be my guest," said Torin, gesturing to the map.

Before Henry could work out another route, he felt the ground shake as a herd of two-legged raptors emerged from the trees. They were Utahraptors, strong and sleek. An armoured warrior rode each raptor. The warriors carried swords on their backs, and had crossbows trained on the Dino Knights. The warriors wore ornately carved helmets that hid their faces. Henry felt his insides melt with fear.

"The little one has the right idea," said a woman's voice. "Steer clear of here."

"Little one?" said Henry, feeling both scared and a bit insulted.

A woman in a black dress came out of the thicket of trees, riding elegantly on her dino. Her hair was dark and well groomed, and perched on top of her head was a diamond tiara that glowed red, reflecting the pulsing volcano above.

"Your Majesty," said Torin. He bowed as well as he could on the back of his dinosaur, and motioned for the others to do the same.

"Majesty?" wondered Henry out loud. He had heard stories about the terrifying

queen who ruled over Volcanica. "Are you Queen Ignis?"

The lady nodded. She carried no weapons, and yet from the way she sat tall on her dino, Henry could tell that she was in charge of the warriors.

"Why are you Brecks invading Volcanica?" demanded the queen, looking straight at Henry.

Henry tried to choose his words carefully. There were rumours that Queen Ignis knew dark magic.

"Your Majesty," began Henry. "We are indeed the Dino Knights of Brecklan. And we seek your forgiveness for our trespass, but we are not invading. Our patrons have been taken by Pterosaurs from the south. We are on a rescue mission."

"That amuses me." She smiled. "And what of Lady Anwyn?"

"Also taken, ma'am," said Torin.

Queen Ignis laughed so loudly that the Utahraptor next to her almost bolted.

"What's funny about that?" asked Ellie.

"She always thought she was so much better than…" The queen's words dried up as a new thought appeared to occur to her. "Taken by Pterosaurs, you say? Hmm…"

"Speaking of which – look!" Gally called from the rear of the group. He pointed upwards, and sure enough, Henry saw the familiar form of Pterosaurs soaring through the sky. He'd never mistake them for birds again – he knew their dark shape now. But this time there weren't just two of them!

"Sir Neville's air force," said Queen Ignis.

Henry counted quickly – twelve of them. Then he heard the sound of arrows sliding across polished wood. The Dino Knights were aiming their crossbows up into the sky.

"Do not engage," the queen said. "Take shelter, instead. Go, now!"

On her command, her warriors scattered towards the trees, away from the open, exposed land. The Dino Knights followed. Henry found himself next to Queen Ignis, sheltering beneath a large fir tree. "How do you know they're from the Swamp States?" he asked.

"I have spies everywhere in Panterra," said the queen. "Sir Neville is a tyrant and he's been breeding Pterosaurs to create a flying armada. A fleet big enough to conquer all of Panterra. But he will never take Volcanica." Her voice was cold with determination.

She turned her Utahraptor and signalled to her warriors to retreat. "Good luck on your quest, young knight. On this occasion, you are free to cross Volcanica. If you survive."

She sped away into the woods on her raptor, followed by her entire platoon of dino-warriors. The Dino Knights were left alone, beneath the looming shadow of the volcano.

"That was close," said Torin. "We're lucky Queen Ignis hates Sir Neville slightly more than Auntie Anwyn."

The wind whispered through the

trees and Henry couldn't help but feel it was all a bit too quiet. They weren't safe yet.

"Come on," he said. He couldn't stop thinking about how the queen had called him "little". He wasn't that tiny, was he?

They returned to the main road and Henry checked that the sky was clear of Pterosaurs.

"I think we're safe." As soon as the words were out of his mouth, he spotted them. Hiding in the top of the trees. The Pterosaurs screeched as they arced down through the sky, dive-bombing the Dino Knights and their beasts, who scrambled in every direction. Conker tried to swat one away with his boulder-like tail, while Torin pulled out his bow and shot arrows at the fearsome creatures.

Gally unsheathed his sword and sliced it through the air.

"Take shelter in here!" called a scratchy voice.

Henry scanned the base of the volcano and spotted the mouth of a dark cave.

"Into that cave!" he called and Rex charged towards it. The others followed.

But Henry pulled on Rex's reins when two red, glowing eyes appeared in the gloom before him. Had he just led them into another trap?

VIII

The red eyes moved closer, growing larger and more demonic. There was a sort of creaking and clanking sound, and then into the light stepped the giant, scaly foot of a Triceratops. In the saddle was a man who ducked beneath the cave roof.

The clanking sounds came from the beast's joints.

Understanding slowly dawned. It was…it was…

"A mechanical beast!" Henry whispered. He couldn't believe what he was seeing. The mechasaur had a patchwork of dino hides for skin, and between the seams Henry saw what looked like the frame of an iron skeleton.

The man didn't introduce himself. "The only chance you have to survive is in here," he said, turning his mechanical monster back into the gloom of the cave.

They ducked inside, just as a Pterosaur swooped down, its savage jaws snapping at them. That was too close. The Dino Knights looked round at each other.

What choice did they have? The mechasaur's eyes lit the way with a spooky red glow, and Henry and the knights followed the stranger down a long, winding tunnel.

They rounded a corner and emerged into another cave, brightly lit by a string of glowing glass orbs that hung from the ceiling. Ellie reached out to touch one. "Ouch!" She snatched her fingers back. "How do they get the candle in there?"

"Magic," said Torin.

"No," said Iyla. "Science."

"That is correct," said the man, smiling to himself. It felt as though Iyla had just passed some sort of test.

He climbed off his mechanical monster, and Henry and the knights dismounted their dinos.

92

"What is that?" asked Gally, staring at the metal dinosaur.

The man gave his machine a firm whack on the head. The mechasaur's red eyes faded as it powered down.

"It looks like more science to me," said Henry. The Dino Knights glanced around the vast cave.

Next to the walls lay tools and vices, worktables and discarded metal contraptions. In the centre of the cave sat a cauldron, filled with a green liquid bubbling away over a fire.

"Science is the future," their new friend said, his voice animated. He was older than Lord Harding, with round glasses, and long white hair that fell onto a grease-stained brown cloak. "Panterra is changing. The land is shifting. Times are moving. The age of the dinosaur is coming to an end and soon it will be the dawn of the machine."

"I don't think so," said Henry. He couldn't imagine a world without dinosaurs.

"And it will all come from this laboratory," he said. "From me."

"But who are you?" asked Torin.

Iyla stepped forward and looked deep into the old man's eyes. "Salterius," she said.

"Hello, Iyla," the old man said with a gentle smile. "You're so grown-up now."

"But you went missing!" she said.

"I'm very much found," he replied.

"Is he dangerous?" asked Ellie.

"No, he's a genius!" Iyla said. "He used to advise the lord on scientific matters."

"Until Harding no longer liked what I had to say," Salterius said. He sat down and pressed a button on a metallic box that sat on the worktable. A small mechanical spider crept over to him, climbed up his leg and hopped on the table. A hose unfurled from its body and squirted hot brown liquid into a dirty mug. "Tea, anyone? No milk, I'm afraid, but I am working on a mechanical cow..."

Henry put his weapon away and nodded to the rest of the Dino Knights to do the same. He gathered them around and spoke in a whisper, while their dinos lay down against the warm volcanic wall to rest and snooze.

"Can we trust him?" Henry asked.

"He's a well-meaning man, believe

me," said Iyla. "He used to make things for Brecklan. But one year there was a bad crop of Brecklan berries and the dinosaurs grew restless, unstable. His wife was killed in a stampede. He started saying to Lord Harding that all dinos were dangerous. He said he could make something better that didn't rely on taming terrible lizards."

Henry looked back to the old man sipping tea. A sadness lay behind his smile.

"After that he was ordered to leave Brecklan," continued Iyla. "No one saw him again."

Henry turned to the old man. "Salterius?" he asked. "You really think mechanical animals can take the place of dinosaurs?"

Salterius lit up with excitement. "Oh, yes! The benefits of automatic mobile mechanoids are many! I did present a paper to Lord Harding, but he didn't seem to like it."

"Let me guess," said Gally. "Because mechanical dinosaurs don't need Brecklan berries?"

"And berries are Brecklan's main trade," continued Henry. "The province would lose lots of money."

Salterius nodded and clapped his hands. A metal pole lowered itself down from the ceiling and he peered through a small eyepiece.

"The Pterosaurs are gone," he said.

Henry approached Salterius and shook his hand.

"Thank you. How can we repay you?"

"No need!" He smiled. "Just tell Lord Harding and Lady Anwyn that my offer of a mechanized dino army still stands."

"If we find them," said Ellie quietly.

"Find them?" Salterius frowned, and Henry quickly filled him in on the kidnapping.

"Harding and I don't agree on much, but I would never want harm to come to him or Lady Anwyn," said Salterius when Henry had finished. "I may have something for you."

He went to the back of the cave and appeared again with a large weapon. It was made of welded steel, with a wooden butt and a long barrel.

"What is that heap of junk?" said Gally.

Did he always have to be so mocking? Henry thought.

Salterius spun around to Gally and pulled the trigger. A rope net burst from the barrel and wrapped itself around the knight, who shrieked like a baby Brontosaurus.

Henry couldn't stop laughing.

"My net-thrower!" said Salterius proudly. "Excellent for dinosaurs. And humans, of course."

Iyla and Ellie attempted to untangle Gally from the net.

"Thank you for your help," said Henry.

He moved to where the dinosaurs were resting. They were sleeping close to each other, tails overlapping, like a pack of giant puppies. Henry roused a warm and sleepy Rex, and couldn't help noticing his battle scars.

"Stay safe out there," said Salterius.

"Panterra is overrun with beasts now, but it won't always be that way."

The Dino Knights followed the path back out of the cave, with Salterius calling farewell. They stepped outside and continued southwards.

After a while, their dinos' feet began to sink into the boggy ground. They had finally reached the Swamp States.

"What a charming province," said Iyla. "I like the way the sunlight ripples off the plumes of gas."

"Is that what that smell is?" asked Ellie. "I thought it was Gally."

They laughed. Everyone was tired, but they had to press on. Torin guided the team around the edge of a swamp.

"What exactly are we looking for?" asked Ellie.

"Maybe that," said Henry, pointing to a stone castle that loomed over the flat swamplands. At the top turret, Henry spotted Avingdon's Pterosaur perched like a bird guarding a nest.

"Avingdon Castle," said Torin, staring at the turrets that touched the grey sky.

Even shrouded in spirals of smoke, Henry could tell the castle was going to be impossible to break into.

IX

Avingdon Castle was built on an island entirely surrounded by murky water. Entry could only be made after crossing two drawbridges. As the Dino Knights drew closer, they could see that each bridge was guarded by a platoon of soldiers, many riding heavily armoured dinosaurs.

"There's too many of them," said Gally. "We should quit while we're ahead."

"We're not ahead, Gally," snapped Ellie.

"And Dino Knights don't quit," added Iyla.

"We'll have to fight our way across," said Torin.

Henry gulped. He'd trained for a tournament, not for combat. "Okay, so then we ride…"

"For Brecklan!" they responded in unison.

The Dino Knights drew their swords and steered their dinos onto the first bridge. As soon as the guards spotted the knights, they swung their staffs and spears. At first, Rex recoiled at the sight of the weapons.

"Give them a fright, Rex," Henry urged, coaxing his beast on.

Rex gathered himself, then let out a tyrannical roar, stopping the soldiers in their tracks. But they didn't retreat.

"Now, knock them down like skittles."

The Tyrannosaur swiped his head at the guards, sending them into the moat in an explosion of water. With the first bridge cleared, the knights pressed on. But the other guards had seen what had happened to their comrades and quickly raised their drawbridge.

"We're stuck," said Gally. "Now is it time to go home?"

"No!" the others replied.

"How can this get any worse?" he asked.

A loud screech answered his

question. From above, Henry spotted Avingdon's Pterosaur dive-bombing to attack.

"Iyla, the net-thrower!" Henry called. "Can you catch that Pterosaur?"

"Maybe!" Iyla hurriedly mounted the net-thrower on Conker's back and aimed it at the sky. As the winged beast barrelled down on them, Henry urged patience. She'd need to release the net at just the right moment.

"Wait, wait, wait…now!"

Iyla pulled the release lever and the net flew up and snagged its prey. The Pterosaur screeched and screamed as her wings caught up in the net and she plummeted to the bridge. The Dino Knights surrounded the captured animal who thrashed in her rope prison.

Henry leapt off Rex and strode towards her. He looked the beast in the eye.

"I'm not going to hurt you, Zia," he said, holding up his hands. The animal stopped flailing. As she lay there, waiting to discover her fate, something inside Henry awoke: a feeling of closeness with this strange beast.

Henry reached for the netting and slowly pulled it off.

"Are you crazy, Henry?" shouted Gally. "She'll snap you in two."

But the Pterosaur simply shook off the rest of the net and let Henry stroke her smooth beak. Henry put his hand on the animal's neck, felt her grey skin heave up and down with each breath. "Nice to meet you, Zia. I'm Henry."

There was no point frightening the

animal any more – no matter how huge and evil-looking she was. It wasn't the Pterosaur's fault that she had been set to work attacking the Dino Knights. Slowly, Henry clambered on her back and leant forwards, gently wrapping his arms around the Pterosaur's neck.

"Amazing," gasped Torin.

"I'm going to fly to the turret. You guys figure out how to get that drawbridge down."

Zia climbed to her feet, flapping her wings, and launched into the sky. Henry felt the wind whip at his face as he tightly gripped the creature's throat. He couldn't believe he was actually soaring through the sky!

The giant dino circled around the castle and descended towards the turret.

It was as though she knew where Henry wanted to be taken. As she banked in the air, Henry spotted a vast field on the opposite side of the castle. It was filled with hundreds of Pterosaurs. Each animal wore an iron collar linked to a chain that was staked into the ground.

"Neville's air force," he gasped. "Queen Ignis was right."

Zia touched down on the top of the turret. It was a graceful landing and Henry slid off her back. He stroked her neck tenderly and thanked her.

"Can you wait here?" he asked.

Zia squawked in agreement.

Henry ran down the circular stone stairway leading from the roof. It was dark but every now and then he'd see a door leading off the stairwell. He paused, gasping, when he spotted the light of a flickering candle and heard the sound of voices. Someone was here.

"You're right, my darling, we cannot give in to his demands," came a familiar voice. Lord Harding!

Henry didn't waste a second. He bounded into the chamber where he found Harding and Anwyn tied to high-backed wooden chairs. There was a blaze roaring in the fireplace and a rectangular hole through which he could see the flock of chained-up Pterosaurs below.

"Henry!" gasped Lady Anwyn. "You came!"

"We all did, my lady," said Henry with a slight bow.

Lord Harding gave Henry a nod and an approving smile. "Well done, lad."

Henry didn't waste a moment. He cut them free with his sword and then turned to lead them out of the chamber. But there stood Neville Avingdon, framed in the doorway. Henry froze to the spot.

"How very cute," Neville said. "This child has come to save you, Harding?"

"This young man is a Dino Knight," replied the lord.

Henry didn't hesitate. He placed himself between Neville Avingdon and his masters and drew his sword.

"The Dino Knights have your castle surrounded. Let Lady Anwyn and Lord Harding go, or we will attack," he said. He was lying, of course, but hoped he was doing it well enough that Sir Neville would not try to test him.

"We're surrounded, you say?

Completely?" said Neville, walking over to the window. "Then I must thank you."

From inside his cape, he brought out a staff.

Henry wielded his sword but Sir Neville simply put the narrow tube to his mouth and blew. A low droning noise floated out through the air.

"Thank you, dear boy!" Sir Neville said again. "I had begun to wonder whether my plan was going to work. I just needed someone foolish enough to take the bait."

"Bait?" repeated Lady Anwyn, the blood draining from her face.

From outside, Henry heard the clinking sound of chains and the now familiar beating of wings. He rushed to the window to see the entire flock of

Pterosaurs take to the sky, each carrying an armed rider on its back.

"Oh no," said Henry, anger rising inside him. He suddenly understood what was going on. He hadn't been part of a rescue mission after all. He had been part of a trap. "The Dino Knights are here, leaving Brecklan totally unprotected!"

Henry turned and looked up at the grey sky above the swamplands filled with hundreds and hundreds of Pterosaurs flying north towards Brecklan.

The attack was on.

"**D**on't be so sure," said Lady Anwyn. "Our brave knights have a plan, don't you, Henry?"

Henry turned back to the lord and lady. His plan only extended as far as rescuing them. He hadn't counted on Sir Neville's treachery.

"We need to go – now!" he said, heading for the stairwell. Perhaps he'd get an idea on the way up to the roof.

Neville Avingdon laughed. "I hope you Brecks can fly."

Henry pushed Sir Neville aside with the flat of his sword. Neville stumbled and Henry snatched the strange instrument that he'd used to call the Pterosaurs. Whilst Neville got back to his feet Henry led Harding and Anwyn out of the chamber and they raced up the stone stairwell, two steps at a time. Eventually, they spilt out of the turret, gasping.

Zia squawked, still waiting for them, just as she'd promised.

Lord Harding froze, placing an arm in front of Lady Anwyn as if that would keep her safe. But Henry scrambled onto the Pterosaur's back. With a wave, he beckoned them to join him.

Anwyn leant into her husband, staring at Henry in a strange way. He just heard her whisper, "Perhaps the legend is true."

What did she mean? But before Henry could ask, Neville burst out of the stairwell with his sword drawn.

"Get off her!" he yelled. "She's mine!"

It was now or never. Harding and Anwyn scrambled onto Zia's back and Henry tapped her neck gently to signal her to take off.

He looked back at Neville for one last time. "Maybe you should have treated her better. Zia, fly!"

Zia rose into the air, giving a squawk of delight. She glided away from the turret and plunged between the other Pterosaurs still filling the sky around them. Far below, Henry spotted the Dino Knights swashbuckling their way across the bridge, knocking the last of the guards into the water as they reached the castle. At last, they were through! Above, the great wings of the Pterosaurs whooshed as they flew northwards to conquer his home.

Zia carried the trio down to the Dino Knights who were now at the main entrance to the castle. Torin and Ellie had their swords drawn.

"It's okay!" Henry called, hopping off the Pterosaur. "She's with me."

"And we're with him," said Lady Anwyn, gracefully climbing down.

Rex had joined the knights and let

out a roar. Was he feeling jealous? Henry stroked his side.

"Henry?" called Iyla. She ran up and flung her arms around him. Henry, embarrassed, returned the hug. "I'm so glad you're all right."

She pulled away and gave a slight bow to Lord Harding and Lady Anwyn. "And you, my lord, my lady."

"We may be safe for now," said Lord Harding, "but Brecklan is unprotected."

"There is a flying armada of Pterosaurs heading north," explained Henry. "It was all part of Sir Neville's plan."

"We saw them in the sky!" Torin said.

"Where is the moustached monster?" said Ellie. "I want to teach him a lesson." She swung her sword in anger.

"A Dino Knight does not exact vengeance," said Harding. "But there will be time to deliver justice once Brecklan is safe."

"We'll never get to Brecklan in time to stop the attack," said Ellie.

"But I can," said Henry. He walked back to Zia and climbed onto her back. Rex let out a sulky groan and looked down at Henry with large, sad eyes.

"Catch me up, buddy," he said, patting the T-Rex fondly. "You guys ride to Brecklan, I'm going to fly after that air force."

Zia launched herself into the sky. Henry grabbed hold of the Pterosaur as she swooped into the air, caught a current and rose high above the clouds.

Zia flew with incredible speed.

Henry kept his head low, gripping on as hard as he could as the clouds scudded past. They swerved left and right, looking for the Pterosaurs until – there! The menacing black shapes of his enemies could be made out, their riders carrying spears or swords.

He couldn't let them reach his beloved Brecklan.

Henry reached for Neville's strange wooden instrument and blew into the mouthpiece as hard as he could. Hadn't Neville used this to summon the Pterosaurs? Maybe Henry could do the same! The low sound filled the sky, and Henry hoped it would be enough to stop the attack.

But nothing happened.

"Get closer," Henry urged.

Zia dived underneath the flock and flew fast enough to get out in front of them. Henry urged her to turn and face them head on. Once again, he blew into the instrument.

But the attacking air force only flew closer, closing in around him. Henry could glimpse the evil that shone in the eyes of the armoured riders. He thought he heard one of them laugh.

"Why are they doing this?" he wondered. "They don't have to listen to Neville. They could be free."

Zia screeched, as if to answer.

And then one of the attacking beasts squawked back. And then another.

The flock of Pterosaurs were barrelling down on them, but suddenly stopped in the sky.

Zia opened her long beak and let out another high-pitched sound.

Understanding prickled beneath Henry's skin. His arms tightened around his companion. "Are you talking to them?"

Each Pterosaur called back with its own reply, until the sky was filled with an overwhelming chorus of the strangest song Henry had ever heard. They didn't sound angry or hostile, they sounded jubilant. Almost as though they were glad to taste the freedom Henry had taken for granted his entire life.

As the animals hovered in the air, the lead beast suddenly threw its rider from its back. The soldier fell through the air, crying out in horror, to plunge into the swamp and disappear beneath the mud. One by one, the other Pterosaurs followed suit. They each bucked their soldiers off until they were all free. Not a human was left in the sky – other than Henry.

"They've freed themselves," he said, amazed at what had just happened, "because of you." For some reason, his new companion had been able to commune with them and talk them round, when he could not.

Zia glanced back over her shoulder at Henry. The two of them gazed into each other's eyes and for a moment it felt as though she could sense what he was telling her. *Thank you.*

As one, the flock banked to the east. Then they split up into smaller groups and separated off in different directions.

Going to their natural homes, Henry guessed. Soon, it was just Zia and Henry.

Henry guided Zia north. Together, they flew over the southern border of Brecklan and soared above the forests until Henry spotted the familiar shape of Harding Manor.

"Can you set us down there?" Henry asked. Zia swooped low over the lawn that was now cleared of the tournament stands. Henry's herd of dinos was out grazing and he was happy to see Bounce with them.

"Hello, everybody!" Henry called from above.

The dinosaurs recoiled at the sight of the winged creature, but as Zia touched down Henry waved again and smiled, to show them they had nothing to fear.

Bounce approached and Henry

gave his old friend a good scratch until Bounce chirped with delight.

Soon, Henry heard galloping behind him and turned to see the Dino Knights and Rex run into the paddock. They were home! Sitting on Conker with Iyla was Lady Anwyn, and Lord Harding rode with Ellie on Kayla, the Styracosaurus. They all quickly dismounted and ran over to join Henry.

"How did you stop the air assault?" asked Torin.

"I'm not sure I did," Henry said. "But I don't think we have to worry about an attack from above any more."

"We spotted Neville riding after us, just a little way behind. He should be here any minute," said Ellie.

Galliard laughed. "I imagine he's

come to see how his invasion is going! He may be in for a surprise…"

They heard claws clattering and Sir Neville charged into the grounds of Harding Manor on an Albertosaurus. The dino walked on two legs like Rex, but was smaller.

"Impossible!" he yelled, glancing around. "Where's the destruction? Why are you all still alive? I bred my Pterosaurs to be ruthless."

Henry folded his arms. "Maybe you should have earned their trust instead."

"Your plan has failed," said Lord Harding. "Now get out of Brecklan. Crawl back to your swamp and never return."

Neville turned his dinosaur around and galloped away, before Lord Harding had time to change his mind about letting him go.

"We should capture him!" Ellie cried. "What if he tries to invade again?"

Lord Harding shook his head. "Leave him," he said. "We are better than that. Avingdon is a proud man, and his shame at losing will keep him stewing in his swamp."

"Where he belongs," added Iyla.

Harding nodded. "Brecklan is safe, thanks to you knights." He paused before reaching out a hand to Henry. "Thanks to you, young lad."

Henry smiled and Lady Anwyn stepped forward to hug him.

"The boy we saved, and now you have saved Brecklan," she whispered in his ear. When she pulled back to look into his face, tears glistened in her eyes. "Thank you."

XI

Henry couldn't eat another bite. The feast had lasted for hours. All the people of Brecklan Town had come back out from hiding in their houses. They were safe again! Lord Harding and Lady Anwyn gave a toast to the knights and singled out Henry for his bravery. The attention made him blush, but he was happy that his team considered him to be one of them. *His* team.

Although he felt part of something, he was still troubled by the fact that his ability – his gift with the dinosaurs – set him apart from his new friends. The dinosaurs listened to him in a way they didn't with other humans. The past few days had proved that to be true. That made him different. Too different?

Lord Harding announced he was going to walk the perimeter of the castle grounds before bed. Henry had often spotted Harding walking the grounds of the estate late at night. This time, he asked if he could come too.

"Do you know anything about my parents, my lord?" Henry blurted. The words were out the moment they left the

manor house. He couldn't hold them in any longer.

Lord Harding took a deep lungful of the cool night air. "I'm afraid not. You were found in the forest as a very young child, no more than two. You were brought to Brecklan Town for safety."

Henry had no memory of this. "Was I all by myself?" That would explain the ache that still sat in his heart. Would it ever go away?

As they rounded the edge of the pasture, the moon shone bright above them. Lord Harding turned his face away, as though he didn't want Henry to see his expression.

"Not exactly, Henry. Did you know the forest dwellers have a legend? They tell of a baby who was snatched at birth and dropped into a nest of dinosaur eggs. The eggs hatched and that human boy was raised as a dinosaur."

Henry thought he understood what Lord Harding was trying to tell him. "Was that boy me?"

Lord Harding gave a noncommittal grunt. "We found you playing with a flock of raptors. At first we thought you were in danger, but as we drew closer we realised that you were almost… How do I say this? One of them."

Perhaps this explained Henry's special connection with dinosaurs.

"It would certainly explain your gift," said Lord Harding, as though he were reading Henry's thoughts. "But be wary, Henry. You only lived in their nest as a baby, and time passes. This ability may wear off as you grow older."

Henry had never thought of himself becoming older. In fact, he had no idea how old he was now! But Lord Harding was right. Henry shouldn't take his gift for granted.

Lord Harding turned back towards the manor, his false leg shining in the moonlight. "I'll leave you here," he said, glancing up at the stars. "Good night."

They'd arrived near the stables. Henry watched his leader walk away – the man who had rescued him and given him a home.

He heard the familiar grunting and snorting from the stables, the dinosaurs hoping for a Brecklan berry. Henry didn't have any of those, but the noises gave him an idea. He crept back into the dining hall and gathered as much leftover food as he could carry. Then he made his way back to the stables and parcelled out the food to the herd in their pens. They squealed and grunted with pleasure.

Henry knew he had a much nicer bed waiting for him in the knights' quarters, with pillows and a soft mattress. He'd earned his right to sleep there. But for tonight, he wanted to be around old and trusted friends. Exhaustion suddenly overwhelmed him. He gave a wide yawn, slowly climbed the ladder, and threw his weary body down on the thin straw mattress.

He gazed down over the animals, including Bounce in the far stall. As he listened to their slow breathing, he knew that he would always be a stable boy.

But as he reached to blow the candle out, there was one other thought that swirled around inside his mind: *I'm also a Dino Knight.*

He closed his eyes. He'd sleep well tonight – or, at least, he hoped so. Because somewhere out there was Neville. And Henry had a feeling their enemy hadn't finished with them yet.

Dinosaur-spotting in Panterra
A PRACTICAL FIELD GUIDE
by Henry Fairchild
Stable Boy, Dino Knight

There are many types of dinosaurs to be found in Brecklan, and even more roaming across Panterra.

Some of them have names almost as big as the animals themselves. And some of those names can be hard to say and even harder to spell. So, I've decided to create a field guide to the dinosaurs you are likely to see in Panterra, including help on how to pronounce their names.

Good luck dino-spotting!

Albertosaurus *(Al-bert-oh-sore-us)*
Smaller than the T-Rex, but no less fierce,
the meat-eating Albertosaurus is Sir Neville
Avingdon's preferred mount when he rides
instead of flies.

Ankylosaur *(Ank-ee-lo-sore)*
The Ankylosaur is a low, solid animal
covered in thick, spiky scales. The
Ankylosaur has a deadly tail that can knock
other dinosaurs sideways. Iyla's dinosaur is
of this kind, and is called ***Conker***.

Deinonychus *(Die-non-i-cuss)*

This dinosaur is one of the many types of raptor and is used by Krilla and her army.

Hypsilophodon *(Hip-sill-oh-fo-don)*

This dinosaur walks on two legs and has scales. The Hypsilophodon is a herbivore and likes to eat Brecklan berries.

Nothronychus *(Noth-ron-ee-chus)*
Torin's dino, called ***Haringey***,
stands on two legs and has
feathers that look a bit like
fur from a distance.

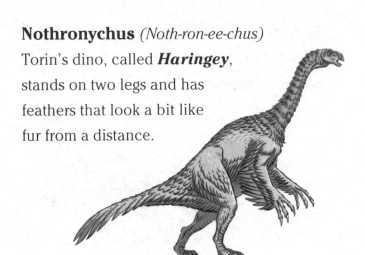

Ornithomimus *(Orn-ith-oh-mim-us)*
A fast, agile dinosaur that can gallop on
two legs and looks a bit like an overgrown
bird. Galliard calls his animal ***Avin***.

Parasaurolophus *(Pair-a-sore-ol-oh-fuss)*

This dinosaur has a hollow horn atop its head that is used for making sounds. These are Lord Harding's preferred animals for pulling his carriage because he likes the horn-sounds they make when they announce his arrival.

Pterosaur *(Tear-oh-sore)*

A winged creature, but not strictly a dinosaur. Sir Neville Avingdon was breeding an air force of these flying beasts.

143

Styracosaurus *(Sty-rah-co-sore-us)*
This dino has six spikes on its head.
This is Ellie's dino,
called **Kayla**.

Triceratops *(Try-ser-a-tops)*
A lumbering herbivore (plant-eater) that
has three horns on its head. My favourite
Triceratops is called **Tribus**.

Tyrannosaurus Rex
(Tie-ran-oh-sore-us Rex)

A large, fierce carnivore (meat-eater).
T-Rexes are known to roam wild in
Panterra, and nobody believed they could
be tamed.

Utahraptor *(You-tah-rap-tor)*

This dinosaur is a raptor. Raptors are very
intelligent and hunt in packs. They are the
choice of the Royal Guardians of Volcanica.

ACKNOWLEDGEMENTS

This book comes from a very special place: *play*.

Torin, the real Torin, my son, was a young boy and was awake in the night and wanted to play. As we lay on our tummies playing with his toys, I placed one of his plastic knights atop a toy dinosaur. Maybe it was the lack of sleep, maybe it was the compelling visual of a valiant knight riding a toy T-Rex, but in that moment, *Dino Knights* was born.

I sketched a crude picture of the pairing and in the days that followed, composed the characters, story and story-world that would become the book you now hold in your hands.

Lots of people helped along the way. Dan Metcalf helped get the story started, Catherine Coe edited an early draft, Karen Ball pushed me creatively to make the story stronger, and Matt Ralphs provided ninja-swift copy editing.

146

Ingrid Selberg believed in the story enough to help publish it independently. I toured the book to schools and young readers were enthralled by the adventure. And so the time came to republish the book with a proper publisher. Sarah Pakenham of Scallywag Press fell in love with the *Dino Knights* and championed a new look, with incredible illustrations from Jeff Crosby, and a whole new publishing program. She and her team at Scallywag have been tireless in their efforts to bring the Knights of Panterra to life.

On the home front, I want to thank my wife, Sidonie, for her continued support and encouragement, Caden for showing me how much fun reading can be, and Torin for being the unknowing inspiration for this series.

Lastly, I need to thank you, the reader. You have so many choices of books and other entertainment to choose from, it means the world to me that you decided to give *Dino Knights* a chance. I hope you enjoy it!

DINO KNIGHTS

Look out for book two
INVASION OF PANTERRA

When a group of exhausted refugee children including Ellie's cousin Caden arrive from the Highlands, telling how masked warriors abducted their families and destroyed their village, Lord Harding believes that Brecklan is likely to be invaded next! The Dino Knights are ordered onto patrol duty to assume the role of protectors. But Henry and Ellie know that the abducted Highlanders need their help, and they take matters into their own hands, launching a secret rescue mission into the treacherous mountains above Brecklan. Without the support of their team, the duo and their dinosaurs risk everything to save Ellie's family.